MELODIES
OF MIDNIGHT

34 DARK TALES

DAVID A. VOLPE

Copyright © 2017 David A. Volpe

Cover/Interior Design by: Ida Fia Sveningsson.
Find her at www.idafiasveningsson.se

CONTENTS

FOREWORD

Certain stories are connected.
Please turn to the "Connecting the Dots" page at
the end of the book when you're finished to see
which stories relate.

INTRODUCTION

What lies ahead are 34 tales of horror and despair.
Step forward into the darkness. Before you go,
remember one thing...nothing is ever as it seems.

Welcome to Melodies of Midnight.

1

BLUE EYES

"I love you and I always will. You have to know that…"
He exhales, "…Those eyes." She peers up at him. "Yes,
those ones. That's what first drew me to you. I knew
it the instant my eyes met yours that I had to have
you… and here we are. I think they call that fate.
Wouldn't you agree?"

Her pale, blue eyes glossed over as he gently
runs his thumb down her cheek. "But like they say,
all good things must come to an end." Lowering her
eyes, she blinks and a single tear drops to the ground
beneath her. He seamlessly interjects at the sight of
the droplet– "No, no, no, don't be sad. What we had
was a once in a lifetime, serendipitous miracle. My
love, our love, will echo into eternity…this I truly
believe."

She remains silent. A strand of hair falls in front of her eye. He simultaneously brushes it behind her ear as he drops to a bended knee while his eyes well up. "We've been together for five years. Don't you have anything to say before we depart? Say anything..." The sincere desperation for a response is apparent in his voice as the silence lingers, and leers at her with a furrowed brow.

She slowly raises her head and nods in agreement. He smiles as he delicately peels the tape from her once beautiful, pink, and supple lips; now cracked and dry. She spits nothing but a whiff of air into his face, "Finally ...I'll be free." She exhales with shallow breath from her dying lips, "You've kept me down here for five years...please... just do it." He places the tape back over her mouth as he rises to both feet.

She quivers as she feels the frigid grip of death slowly embracing her, but then a smile creases the tape. One final tear descends from her eye. He tightens the rope around her ankles, attached to a cinder block and kisses her forehead, "goodbye my love..." He pushes her down the well.

She lets out a single shriek that echoes for what seems to be an eternity until it fades into nothingness, as does she. "Like I said...echo into eternity." He whispers as he turns away, disappearing into darkness...

2

HUMMINGBIRD

Ding! Text message: "Hey, honey. Remember, Room 107 at 7 pm. Dinner is at 8. Love you <3"

"Can't wait. I love you too," he responds without hesitation. He arrives home just as the sun sets in his rearview.

"Wearing your favorite dress ;)" he reads, as he tightens the Windsor knot to his collar.

"Wearing your favorite suit," he replies.

Glancing up at himself in the mirror, he smiles. A slideshow of flashbacks to their first date, first dance, and their first kiss play in his brain. He breathes in, then exhales as if he were calming himself just before giving a speech in front of a thousand anxious attendees.

The GPS says aloud, "Arrived." He reaches into his pocket, revealing a black velvet box containing a shimmering diamond mounted to a beautiful golden ring. The pace in his step quickens as he strolls down the hallway in excitement.

"107" reads the door. He enters, holding a dozen yellow roses; they're her favorite. The lights are dim and the room is vacant. He peruses the space for a moment finding a note with red lipstick kissed onto the front. He flips it over, "Freshening up... Have a glass of wine." As instructed, he kicks off his shoes, removes his jacket, sits down, and sips the wine placed adjacent to the note.

Ding! Text Message: "Get my note?"

He grins, "I did. Come out here in under a minute and I'll do my signature strip tease."

"You haven't done that for me in years..."

Amused, he responds, "You mean last month for our anniversary...and you say my memory is bad!"

"The last time was the night we met. Remember? You said you liked my hummingbird tattoo as we lay there in bed for those final fleeting moments together..."

His heart drops. Terror engulfs his body. Chills run down his spine and goose bumps cover his arms. The wine slips through his fingers and splashes onto the white carpet. He leaps to his feet only to fall back down. His body felt like a ton of bricks and his eyesight began to blur– fading, fading...black.

His vision refocuses. Only to find himself gagged and tied to a chair facing his bleeding dearest, bound in the same fashion. Her neck had been slashed seconds before regaining his wits. He panics and struggles unsuccessfully trying to reach her, as he peers into the eyes of his dying beloved who stares back hopelessly in horror. Just as the life drains from her body completely– he feels the icy touch of sharpened steel held from behind press against his throat. His gaze whispers, "I love you" as hers' reciprocates the same. He looks down at the hand gripping the blade...a hummingbird tattoo.

"If I can't have you... no one can." The haunting, familiar voice says silently as the knife drags deep and slow across his neck.

3

INTO THE WOODS

"When I say GO, run as fast as you can through the woods. It's a shortcut home. You have to run really fast so he doesn't get you," they say to him.

The new student scrunches his eyebrows in confusion, "So who doesn't get me?"

They explain further. "There's a clown who lives in there, and if you're fast enough, then he won't get you. Just run, okay?"

"Okay," He answers, careful not to ask too many questions out of fear of being teased.

"Ready...Set...Go!" The three sprint down the path. Trees are colored with shades of autumn and leaf covered ground crunches with every step. Thus far, he hasn't seen anyone except for his classmates running with laughter. "There's no clown," he thought.

They just wanted to see if the new kid could keep up.

A warm feeling washes over him as he smiles back; finally, he feels as if he belongs somewhere. About halfway through, they saw the light of the sunset peeking through the trees. "Last one out gets their head shaved!"

He ran like the wind and making it out first, he raises his arms in triumph. "I won!" Another minute passes under the moonlight without an appearance from the others who followed closely upon heel. His voice echoes into the dark forest. "Hey, guys?"

After another dragging minute, he ventures back to find them. A blanket of uneasiness wraps him tightly as he steps forward. He's careful not to make a sound but the leaves crackle like fireworks beneath his feet. He's starting to think that the murderous clown was real after all.

He trips to his hands and knees. Brushing the dirt from his pants, he noticed the bloody rock by his feet. Not far from it laid his friends. Each of their heads was pulverized like ground meat, and their broken teeth were sprinkled around their corpses. A detached eye stared back at him as he trembled with terror.

He jumped to his feet and ran faster than he ever had before.

He bursts through the door and cries, "Mom! Help me! Help! My...my...friends!" Taking a deep breath through his sobbing, he continues, "We ran from the clown in the woods! It was light out and then it got dark all of the sudden. He got them, mom, he got them! "

She sympathetically gazes back at his disorientated face and says, "It's okay. Just breathe..."

He screams, "Did you hear me? They're dead! Both of them...their brains, their faces..." He looks down at his hands and clothes. "...But why am I covered in blood?"

Grabbing both sides of his cheeks, she crouches to his level. "Baby, just breathe with me. You had another blackout. We're going to get through this, just like before. What's the last thing you remember?"

4

CHERRY WINE

"Don't. Please... don't do this," she pleads with the woman in a black dress fixing her lipstick in the mirror.

Ignoring the desperate plea, she nonchalantly answers, "Do you like this shade? It's called..." she glances down at the label, "Cherry Wine."

Tears build with each sharp and angry breath. "We didn't agree on this. I thought this time was different. Why can't you let me be happy?" The silence extends as she awaits an explanation that doesn't exist.

She stomped her heel in punctuation. "I don't know how many times we have to go through this— You might produce a few episodes, but I'm running the show. What I say goes. End of story."

Her smile, hypnotic eyes, and those winding curves in a fitted dress were enough to blind any man from her treacherous intentions. The stale cadavers fertilizing the soil behind her house can surely confirm that.

"Oh, and the poison in his drink is fast acting. Don't waste your precious time in here arguing with me. Bring him home to me when your date is through. If you don't, I'll make you slit his throat with your own hand as you watch the blood spill down his chest. Please, just do as I say. Now wipe your eyes before you go, you look like a hooker in a rainstorm with that bleeding eyeliner."

She dried the tears from her face and kisses her cheek. "That's better."

There's a knocking at the door. "Hey, everything alright in there? It sounded like you were yelling at someone?"

"Yep, all good! Oh, no just talking at my clumsy self...got some soap on my dress," she laughs. "Be out in a sec."

She touched her lips and hair once more before strolling back to her candlelit dinner for two. As the door swings shut, the mirror reflects a vacant bathroom with only the stain of Cherry Wine kissed upon the glass.

5

STATIC

The footsteps grew louder with the passing of seconds. I can hear my heart pounding out of my chest. "Shut up! Shut up! Please God, silence my heart until he leaves," I thought to myself. My trembling hand pressed firmly over my mouth to stifle my labored breathing. "Maybe he'll just take what he wants and leave. Maybe he doesn't know anyone's home. My car has been in the shop and the house is dark," I reassure myself.

"Sssssssssshhhhhhhhhhhhhh!" the sound of static rings out as the TV flashes on. I glance down; my fucking cat just stepped on the remote in the middle of the floor. I look up, only to see the empty void of two soulless eyes staring into mine.

He rips open the slotted closet with ease and a smile. He threw me to the ground and mounts me. He held my throat with one hand and struck my jaw with the other. Stars flash as I leave my body and fall back into it all at once. He hits me again...and again... and again.

My legs fall limp and my breathing grows shallow. I can feel his grip tightening around my neck as those bottomless pits of despair glare down at me with joy and triumph.

As he senses the light diminishing from my fluttering eyes, the reflection in his said something different. Satisfaction turns to sadness and pleasure into pain. Everything changed in that instant, but he knew his role and I knew mine. He blinks and death returns. I couldn't fight him if I tried, I'm not even sure I wanted to anymore so I prepared myself to suffer.

My terror shifts to denial, grief, acceptance, and then nothing. Just a glazed look, as the room grows darker and I feel less and less. The ticking of his watch adjacent to my ear intensifies. Louder and slower simultaneously...tick...tick...tick. His grip loosens as he feels the vitality vacate my limber extremities that fail to struggle. I sensed he wanted to save me, but also to squeeze harder, and he should... after what I did. My only regret...loving him in the first place.

"Sssssssssssshhhhhhhhhhhh," says the static, and I listen.

6

PUPPET MASTER

"Of course he's coming. He's my little puppet; he'll do whatever I say. Me too, can't wait to see you either," she whispers with a smile as she ends the call. "Hey, babe, coming to bed?" she yells toward the bathroom.

"Yes, dear. Be right there," he says cheerfully. "Who was on the phone?" He slides beside her under the covers.

"It was just my mother checking in. So first, we'll go to her house and then wine tasting with Philip and Michelle," she said, facing him in bed.

"Mhm," he sighs, still engrossed in his book.

"You're not even listening. You should probably worry about escaping that cubical at work instead of this conversation. A promotion could give us that pool I want for the backyard." She laughs through her nose at the thought of Michelle's face after seeing a pool superior to hers. He rolls his eyes.

"Roll your eyes all you want. You're lucky I don't leave you for Philip," she said in a snarky tone. "Now that's a man I can stand behind. Just kidding, but did you know he's going to make V.P. this year?"

"...I didn't know that," he says like he cares.

She pulls the sheets up to her chin. "Let's get some sleep. Love you, goodnight."

He kisses her cheek. "Love you too," he says and clicks the bedside lamp collapsing the room to black. She closed her eyes and wraps her arm around his chest. Suddenly, her peaceful sleeping breaths were interrupted by the sound of a drill. A piercing scream follows the noise.

"Sorry to wake you," he says as if he abruptly climbed back into bed after a late night snack. He clicks the lamp on. "So that was your mother on the phone... 'Philip' is a strange way to spell mom, isn't it? I know you two have been fucking behind my back," he calmly says while holding her phone.

Her hands were tied securely to the headboard. He continues drilling holes through her mangled wrists. She hollers uncontrollably as the look of horror emanates from her eyes, staring up at her husband's joyous smile. Black lines trailed down the edges of her lips and blush was patted heavily on her white powdered face. He fastens the thick wires through her gushing wrist holes. "Now you're my little puppet," he snickers as blood cascades down her body, onto their white thousand count sheets.

He unties her hands and her dangling arms fall limp upon the bed. "Dance for me, darling," he laughs as he works her strings.

7

RED CHRISTMAS

Each Christmas Eve, he took his girls to the family cabin to open their gifts at midnight. He and his wife would drink rum-spiked eggnog beside the warmth of a crackling fireplace, while their daughter would play with her new toys to the melodies of holiday classics. He noticed the fire diminishing as the chilly draft swept down the chimney. "Be right back," he said as he began lacing his boots.

His wife sits by the shimmering lights of the tree, sipping her tea in a cozy pink robe. "Hurry, or we'll open the presents without you!"

"You wouldn't dare...fine, just one until I get back with the firewood." His daughter's face lit up as she shook each box to her ear. Things couldn't be more perfect, he thought as he walked out the door and began the trek to the woodshed.

He stacks the wood in his arms as the snow floats onto the frozen forest floor. The porch light shines like the North Star through the white wall of the blizzard. He starts toward his cabin with the bundle in hand. Suddenly, leaves rustling to his left halt the cadence of his steps. His eyes widen and his heart skips a beat. He spins his head in both directions. Only blankets of untouched snow stretched for miles. "Damn squirrels," he chuckled nervously.He continued walking but the snapping of twigs and shifting leaves echo into his ear once more. His heartbeat and foggy breath hasten at the sound. He squints his eyes and just out of focus reveals a silhouette stalking his every move. Its glowing yellow eyes stare directly at him from behind the trees. The jet-black creature creeps closer and breaths in his fear, like blood to a shark. The beast continues to leer a moment longer, then darts after him. Just feet from his heels snap the jaws of death as the distance rapidly closes between them. One final step remains to safety when a crushing weight clamps onto his shin.

The wolf towers over him, dripping hot saliva onto his face as he crawls toward salvation. The only thing between his neck and its razor teeth are his shaking hands desperately holding off its snout. Finally, it lunges and sinks its teeth into his pulsing throat. He gasps for air but chokes on blood as it pools around him. The brilliant white snow instantly darkens into scarlet under the luminescent moon. His hopeless eyes turn to the window. He reaches a yearning arm to his daughter and wife tearing open their gifts with gleeful smiles.

A humanlike figure emerges from the shadows. He slinks closer with slow and steady steps. He strokes the wolf as he stands in the river of blood. He smirks down at him, and then at his family through the frosted glass. "Precious, aren't they?"

His warning call is stifled as he coughs up chunks of blood, failing to belt out their names. His icy tears freeze to his cheek as he takes the memory of their smiles to his snowy grave.

The man in the trench coat and top hat proceeds to grab the door handle but doesn't twist it. He looks back to the snarling wolf awaiting command. "Feed," he says. Its teeth rip and mash his face to nothing but heaps of steaming pulp before devouring the rest of his body.

The muffled sound of "White Christmas" resonates just on the other side of the door. He pulls a long carving knife out from under his coat as he hums the melody of White Christmas under his breath. He throws open the door and stomps his bloody boots into the home at midnight with the girls' final gift gripped tightly in his palm.

8

DINNER PARTY

They sat around the candlelit table and lowered their heads as the host concluded grace. "...And thank you for my lovely new neighbors. I hope you all enjoy this food as much as I enjoyed preparing it. Let's eat."

Excitedly, the guests snatched their silverware and went to work. Mid-way through dinner, a repeating thud is heard from the basement door. The host, whose hair and beard are peppered with gray, ignores it.

It continues. "Thump...Thump, Thump." The guests curiously glance over at each other. "Do you hear that too?" they say with their eyes.

"Thump. Thump. Thump." Furious, the host firmly slams down his wine glass. He quickly regains composure and smiles. "Hey, cool it down there or we won't save you any dessert!" It suddenly stops.

The guest at the far end of the table sighs empathetically. "Kids... am I right?" Everyone laughs at his quip. The sound of silence warms him with joy, as he observes the satisfied faces around the table devouring their meals.

"Wow...this slides right off the bone," another guest adds. "Where do you get your meat?"

"Beautiful, I know," says our host. "It's local. Actually, from right down the street."

"It literally melts in your mouth. It's to die for; almost a shame to eat it." He dips a rib in the bloody marinade collected on his plate. "You might be onto something there with that 'no dessert' comment. There won't be a trace if it's anywhere as wonderful as this meal." They all chuckle in unison.

Bones began clacking on plates as the guests finish licking them spotless. Laughter ensues as the hours grow longer and the wine flows freely. The guests appear to find everything funny tonight; maybe it's because they're nervous. They've never seen wealth like this before. He now owned the largest house on the block, coming complete with marble floors, chefs, maids, and a feast fit for a king. All at once can be awe striking.

Or maybe as they chewed the rubbery fat and picked the tender flesh from their teeth, they were obliviously unaware that the meat was cut from the humans held captive downstairs, and they're next on this week's menu.

9

GOOD SAMARITAN

"Oh my god! Are you okay?" She screams out. The raindrops dancing on the asphalt is the only response reciprocated. The child sat in a puddle with his eyes lowered to the ground. Checking for injuries, she insists that he come with her out of the downpour.

He hasn't yet said a word, but taking her hand, the two drive off. "Do know where you live? Where are your parents?" The boy shrugs his shoulders.

Again she questions, "It's raining terribly and it's dangerous out here. Why were you in the middle of the road?" He doesn't as much as shrug this time.

He finally mumbles something vague. "What was that honey? I didn't hear you?" She glances at him in the rearview mirror staring blankly out the window in a daydream.

"Are you okay? Blink once for Yes and twice for No," she says with a giggle. Pressing his head against the window, he sighs and whispers something once more.

She raises her eyebrows and reaches back, touching his knee in comfort. "I'm a nurse. You can trust me. I help kids like you every day. Are you in pain? Is that why you can't speak to me?"

She climbs into the backseat to better hear what's stuck under his breath. "...In your ear?" She points to her ear as if she's solving her partner's sentence in charades. "Ah!" She exclaims, "Something hurts in your ear! Let me see..."

The rain taps on the roof as rolling thunder rumbles in the distance of dusk. She tilts her head to check his ear as their cheeks nearly brush. He stared into her eyes, then at her neck. "Right under the ear," he says and digs his teeth into her jugular.

Blood sprays the back windshield as she tries to plug the leak with her fingers. His pupils reflect hysteria in the woman's dying eyes. The blood continues to ooze generously from her throat.

He smiles at the sight, licking his sharpened teeth. A horn beeps and high beams flash from behind, illuminating the boy's blood dripping mouth. He crawls, hands and feet into the Cadillac with tinted windows.

"Good boy. See, when you bite that vein right under the ear the blood flows beautifully." Says the ominous voice, as they drove past the Good Samaritan's sedan into the midnight blue horizon.

THE DEVIL'S DOOR

He peered up at the monstrous gate before him. Decades of unkind seasons have battered the swirls of handcrafted iron vines—once a deep rich black with golden handles, and now lackluster and decayed with burnt-orange rust.

Green leaves and flowers are vivid with vitality resting behind him; contrary to what laid just yards ahead through the swinging gate—Bare and twisted trees hunched over the cobblestone path as night creatures lurked behind the veil of shadows.

Through the black iron vines and down that rocky road, stood a decrepit house that has earned a sinister reputation. The surrounding town had its fill of disappearances, so they knew to stay far removed from that wretched place. Nevertheless, curious tourists who enjoyed the adrenaline fix of flirting with darkness, often found themselves staring up at that same gate. They say that the house coaxes your deepest fears out of hiding. Your reality will melt down until only terror occupies your mind. The few who have returned refuse to discuss what happened to them. It was once described as if happiness was being siphoned from their veins and replaced with dark tunnels of loss.

As he marvels at the towering gate as his gut screams, "Get Out! Go, now! Turn and never look back." But there's magnetism to it, a seductive secret he was dying to uncover. It pulled him closer until his hand finally touched the cold iron. "Do it. I won't hurt you. I promise," it whispers.

Ones soul cannot hide the secrets of its true desire within the walls of that broken place in the distance. And what they desire is death. Those who are pulled to this place wish to die in one familiar form or another, whether they know it or not. They come here hoping that somewhere under the looming shadow of death's cooling chill, they'll ring in the bravery needed to fight for the life they willingly surrender by opening the devil's door.

"Let's just go. We came, we saw, now let's get the hell out of here. You've heard the stories..." his friend says to him. The suggestion falls upon deaf ears, as the shrieking sound of rusted hinges echo into the night as his hand shoves the gate. Moonlight illuminates the path in which he sets upon, but will never return from. As one foot follows the next, death followed quickly upon heel.

11

AWAKE

The darkness resembled his lightless room, but somehow he knew it didn't feel the same. "It doesn't smell like my sheets," he thinks, inhaling the scent of wood and dirt. He arched his back in discomfort from the unfamiliar surface. "This isn't my bed. Why is there an echo? What the fuck is going on?" Blindly trailing his fingers through the blackness, he feels the hardened surface of the plywood that enclosed him.

Then, it dawns on him with a sudden wave of certainty—I'm in a box.

His chest tightens as the air becomes like boulders stacking themselves higher with every second he lies under their crushing weight. He hyperventilates through the tormenting panic, pushing against the immovable force. He yells, "Help! Help! Can anybody hear me? Help me!" But like a tree that falls in the woods—If nobody's listening, do his screams make a sound?

He wildly punches and kicks, but the wood is a stubborn foe. His hands and feet become more battered and torn with each sorry attempt. The oxygen draws thinner with each withering breath. He violently thrashes as tears begin to run down his temples. Only nubs remain of his splintered fingernails that fail to scratch their way to freedom. His paper white bones peek through the skin of his knuckles as his weakening punches defeatedly strike the blood-soaked wood.

He inhales but chokes on a sliver of air that swallows into his lungs. "Breathe... breath," he thinks, as he gasps at nothing in his airtight coffin.

"Help...help...me," he struggles to whisper. The memory of his mother rocking him to sleep on their porch crept through his brain. He sobs silently and bangs his head with regret. His final moments are met with wishes of burned bridges he now longed to repair.

A final flickering thought of the one who holds his heart; gone like sand sifting through an hourglass, and now only a few grains remain. He whispers, "I love you," as he faded from the world he knew, buried alive in an unmarked grave atop a forgotten hill.

He abruptly sprung to life at the end of his closing exhale. He sucked the fresh air like a vacuum from the comfort of his bed. Sweat beads on his forehead as he grabbed his chest and reaches into the roofless abyss of his room. He sat up and wiped away his tears as he looked to his left, where the flashing red light illuminated "6:00 AM" on his ringing alarm clock.

12

NIGHT SHIFT

"Nobody lasts on the night shift. It's usually one and done for most folks. I've been working it for years. It's kind of nice actually, but to each their own, I suppose," he says as he walks in stride with the new hire.

"Night of the living dead is my favorite movie so I should feel right at home," he replies in a lively tone.

"That's the spirit! Graveyard pun, sorry, occupational hazard," he chuckles. "Okay, here are the keys. Make your rounds every hour on the dot and watch out for kids playing with Ouija boards. It's a big thing around Halloween. They usually bring beer; start kicking things over, you get the picture," he adds and rolls his eyes.

He nods. "Gotcha."

"Great. I'm heading out, just give me a holler if anything comes up."

He toured the cemetery as his manager drove down the winding road. Darkness shrouds the graves as the night reclaims its domain from the sun, who turns your eye from what's hidden behind veils of light.

Silent owls spy from above as he wandered the maze of headstones. Here, time stood still, far removed from the chaotic world of the living. He enjoyed the eerie calmness of the cooling touch of the passing breeze. Suddenly, a long and haunting howl echoes in the distance of the tree line. "There aren't any wolves in these parts," he thought as his pace quickened.

A shadow flashed to his left. He yells at the figure fading into the mist. "Hey! You can't play in here, kid." His heart thumps louder than his footsteps. Then it howls again, but this time closer. His flashlight fails to cut through the thickening fog, reducing him to a blind sitting duck.

There were two freshly disheveled holes just a few feet ahead. He runs to them and stops at the edge before falling in. He looks down at the open coffins containing freshly dismembered corpses with crushed skulls, shredded limbs, and both are disemboweled. The metallic smell of blood and rotting flesh flood his nostrils. He vomits as he falls to his knees and drops the flashlight into the man's gaping chest cavity. "Shit, shit, shit!" He frantically dialed the grounds manager but it goes straight to voicemail.

The figure sweeps back around, bumping him down into guts and bones before vanishing once more. Covered in blood, he begins pulling himself out of the hole but halts at the sound of heavy breathing. The animal stood like a bear, nearly eight feet tall as its exhales steamed into the brisk air.

He lies in the soggy remains and pulls the coffin closed without a sound. He struggles to stomach the stench, as the cold viscera soaked through his clothes and dampened his back. The footsteps dissipate as the monster fades back into blackness.

A loud, "DING!" rings out from his pocket.

The text reads, "Just checking in to make sure the zombie apocalypse hasn't started on your first shift lol! Oh and it's his feeding time, so I hope you completed your rounds by now. I told you we kept a strict schedule."

His heart drops as the casket rips off its hinges and he stares into the gleaming red eyes of death incarnate. It claws into his back like a meat hook and drags him screaming helplessly into the forest never to be seen again.

13

BLACK WIDOW

Twelve stories below the crowded party, the ground sparkled under the street lamps as snowflakes delicately descended. She perused the apartment, intricately minding the art as if she were alone in a private gallery; paying no mind to the babbling silhouettes that surrounded her. One piece in particular especially held her attention. She sat idly on the couch across from the painting of a black widow. She peered deeply into the vibrant red hourglass upon its back as if she were staring at her own reflection.

Breaking her trance, a blonde woman wearing thick rimmed glasses plops beside her and glances up at the spider. "Creepy right, here alone?"

"Beautiful actually...and yes," she says, sipping her drink through her lipstick stained straw.

"A gorgeous girl like you, here without a man... now I've seen everything."

She blushes. "You're too kind, but I prefer it this way. It keeps me young."

The woman threw her head back with laughter. "You can say that again! Mine drives me up the wall." She combed back a handful of hair. "I sprouted another patch of gray this month alone!"

She chuckles through pressed lips. "Which one is your husband?"

She points to him. He notices and waves to them with a friendly smirk.

She catches his lingering gaze, and mischievously smiles back. "He's handsome."

The woman places a hand on her shoulder and smirks. "You can have him, honey. I have to use the restroom. I'll be right back."

She spotted his lustful stare amongst the sea of blurred faces as his wife retreats down the hallway. Her eyes call him over. She catches the scent of his immoral intentions through the thickness of clashing perfumes as he approached. "Hi, I'm Bill," he says smoothly.

She noticed his outstretched hand had the pale impression of a missing wedding ring. "And I'm about to leave." She enjoyed playing hard to get.

He pleads, "Come on, this party's great. Look around, everyone's having fun. Why so blue?"

She looks up at him, then around the room. "Do you ever notice the heaps of bullshit spewing from the mouths of people who never have anything of value to say? Its just noise bouncing between walls, overflowing at the brim with narcissists ear-raping us with never-ending bitching or bragging."

"Wow, are you always this pleasant?" He helped himself to the open seat adjacent to her and places a hand on her exposed leg. "Just messing, I know what you mean."

"You know what I mean? So if I said that I wanted to escape, would you take my hand?"

"Escape to where?"

She stands to her feet as his eyes trailed the winding curves in her black skin fitting dress. "Would you like to find out?"

Of course, she didn't have to ask twice. Her hips seductively swing as her heels glide through the maze of stiff bodies. Bill follows closely behind with their palms tightly clasped. She led him out the fire escape ascending to the frigid rooftop.

He crossed his arms and rubs his shoulders. "Aren't you cold wearing that?"

She inhales slowly with closed eyes. "I love the smell of crisp winter air. Come sit next to me." Again, he follows suit.

"Whoa, don't look down," he laughs flirtatiously and scoots closer.

She peered out over the edge. "Doesn't it feel like we're sitting at the edge of the world? Up here the sky is blacker and the stars are brighter, nothing quite like it."

The city's busy buzz softened to a gentle whisper below their dangling feet, as ant-sized humans strolled the sidewalks. Her emerald eyes cut through him as she brushed the windblown hair from her face. "When you have two voices in your head pulling you in opposite directions, which do you listen to?

Entranced by her intensity, he leans in. "It depends. What are they saying?" His shivering lips inch closer to hers.

Their noses touch as she reciprocates his advance. "One tells me to do it, the other tells me not to."

His eyes closed as he prepared to taste her sweet lips. "Always listen to the one that says, 'do it.'"

The instant their lips meet, she pulls away. "I always do..." She pushes him from the ledge and smiles as his betrayed stare falls farther from sight. She leaned forward and watched the whole way as he hurtled to the ground. The snowy pavement looked as if she dropped a red-paint filled balloon onto a blank canvas. His body glued to the sidewalk just waiting to stick to someone's shoe.

She rose to her feet, brushed the snow from her dress, and climbed back down to the static of blended voices. One familiar voice cuts through the others as a hand gripped her shoulder. "Hey, have you seen my husband?"

14

LAKE HOUSE

"We did it. Homeowners..." he said and twisted the key into the lock.

"Homeowners—I like the sound of that. Almost as much as 'Mr. & Mrs. Jones,'" she says, glancing down at her wedding ring sparkling in the sunlight.

They began unpacking and sorting the home's contents into boxes. She grabbed a doll that sat in a recliner in front of a wall-sized window, looking out at the vast lake. "Check out this creepy thing." He was dressed in a red shirt, denim overalls, and beady black-buttoned eyes. He had the oddest smile on his face. It looked as if he knew your most intimate secrets.

"Weird, he definitely goes in the 'junk' box." They stowed him in the basement after sorting out the rest of the room. "What about this recliner?" he asks, brushing the dust from its cushions.

"I don't know, I kind of like it." She sinks into the seat. "It's surprisingly comfortable and it gives the room a splash of character. Let's keep it."

They drove into town that night and celebrated at a five-star restaurant with overpriced bubbly. They return to find "put me back," carved into the recliner. "Should we call the cops? What does it even mean?" she says with concern.

"Don't be ridiculous. It's probably some teenagers trying to spook us. We'll get the locks changed," he says and kissed her forehead.

Shortly after, a giggle echoes into their ears as they lie in bed. She nudged his arm and whispers, "Did you hear that?"

He silently holds a finger to his lips. "Probably the same kids who sliced the chair," he says softly. "I'll scare them off."

He wildly charged down the hall but discovered an empty room at the end of it. He opens the front door and quickly scans the perimeter...nothing.

He turned from the door and there he was, sitting in the recliner looking out at the lake with those beady black eyes. Only now, his smile was gone.

He shuffles back to bed and scratches his head. "Nobody's out there, except for the doll...that we put in the basement this morning."

In the days that followed, they threw him out, tossed him in the fireplace, but he mysteriously returned unscathed. The dolls face expressed anger now, and they experienced strange occurrences around the house. They began arguing and keeping secrets. She, in particular began to resent him. They concluded that the only way to stop the madness was to place the doll back in the recliner; things always seemed to calm down after that.

She looked at him with a slight detection of worry. "Maybe we should ask the realtor if she knows anything. She has to know something about this house."

"Good idea, I'll give her a call." He dials the office.

A voice smiles through the phone. "Lakeside Real Estate, this is Sharon. How can I help you?

"Hey, It's Mr. Jones. I own the old house down on the lake. I know this is going to sound insane, but do you know anything about a doll or recliner that came with the house?"

"Hi, there! Ummm, all I know is that it was the previous owners' most prized possession. It was his son's. Sad, what happened to that family," she somberly says.

"What happened to them?"

She pauses. Her voice drops to a chilling whisper. "His wife jumped into the lake with their baby in her arms after he wouldn't stop crying. The husband died just weeks later from a broken heart, sitting in the recliner as he held the doll by his side.

"Don't you have to disclose that to potential buyers?"

"Their deaths were ruled an accident, so technically...no," she snickers.

"Great, thanks for your help," he says sarcastically.

Later that afternoon, his wife frantically rushed over to him relaxing by the dock. He noticed tears dribbling down her cheeks. "What's wrong?

What's wrong?" he asks, jumping to his feet. She flashed a pregnancy test from behind her back.

"We're pregnant? I love you," he whispers and pulls her close.

The passing months provided peaceful slumbers without a single bump in the night. Finally, they were ready to rid themselves of the cursed doll once and for all; so they tied a brick to his ankle sunk him to the bedrock of the midnight green lake. Her water broke that same day.

Every night since the birth, their baby boy wailed and screamed until morning despite their unconditional affection. She hasn't slept a minute in weeks. The only time he stops crying is when she sat with him in the recliner facing that wide-open lake.

On a particularly chilly morning, the winds whipped the water into waves crashing upon the banks. She stood at the edge of the dock with their crying swaddled newborn and peered into the rolling swells. "Hey! What the hell are you doing? Get back from there, that wood is super slick!" he scolds as he runs toward them.

She dangles a foot over the water. Her shoe falls into the sweeping undertow and the baby's blanket is taken with the wind. "Get away from there right fucking now!" he desperately commands. Just out of arm's reach, he outstretches his hand to them. "Take my hand!" he screams. She turns to him and smiles before falling backward and plunging into the water. The violent unforgiving lake swallows both wife and son. So there he lies, soaked and sobbing at the end of the dock staring down at his heart sinking deeper as the tiny blue blanket floats down to his lap.

Weeks passed but time held no meaning. It wasn't day or night, it wasn't early or late; it was simply he without them. He sat in that cracked leather recliner staring out at the lake with his son's blanket wrapped in his arms, hoping to see his family walking home from the dock.

And that's exactly how they found his corpse three months later.

15

WANTED

Among the thousands of spam advertisements and get rich quick schemes, sat one lonely wanted ad that was unlike all the others:

"Subject: I Want to Kill You...

Do you want to die? Does the thought of waking up tomorrow sound so terrible that you wish it could all be over? That's where I come in...

I'm here to help you. You can call me Freedom, pleasure to meet you. Do you feel like prisoner in your own mind? Are you trapped under the weight of darkened thoughts? Let me free you from your pain. You've felt nothing for so long and it's time to finally feel again. You will yearn for life, but only for an instant before I snuff out that spark in your eye.

I want to make you scream. I want to manifest your worst nightmares and drag your deepest fears into the light. So tell me, what frightens you? What makes you fear the dark? Tell me all about the things that keep you up at night. Intrigued? Still reading? Good. See text below for more information...

Terms & Conditions:

1. I will kill you in any way it pleases me. I won't be scooping out your organs and going through all this work just to bury you in an overpriced bed like your family would do to you. No, you will receive the respect and care that you deserve. A hunter must honor his prey. Picture this—It's Saturday night and I'm sipping your blood like wine as I wear your face and cook your seasoned body to Mozart. Not a piece of you will go to waste. This is your night and you deserve my undivided attention.

2. If you like games: I've built a maze for you to escape from. You won't, but you're welcomed to try. I'll provide you with defensive tools in case you get that urge to live again, but they won't be able to help you. This much I promise.

3. Send me your schedule — where you'll be each day at what time. Also, attach your full name and address. Thank you in advance. Don't worry about finding me... I'll come to you. It might not be tomorrow or the next day, but I will come for you. I'll snatch you when you least expect it. There's no fun in a stage act, so I want this to be as organic as possible.

4. If you choose to respond, know that the hourglass has flipped. There's no turning back. Take this time to say your goodbyes because, who knows, tonight you may glace up to the mirror after brushing your teeth only to see my face over your shoulder in your mirror just seconds before I take you. Utilize these last moment wisely; I don't want you having any regrets. But please, do not stray from your schedule.

If this sounds like something you might be interested in, then reply to this posting with the subject head, "I'm Ready," and we'll get started. Hope to hear from you soon!

Sincerely, Freedom"

Just as the sun drops and the skies fall dark, a response reads: "I'm Ready..."

16

THE LETTER

He wandered the house one ominous room at a time. The floorboards are thick with dust and the long halls carry a chilling draft as the melting candle wax dripped onto his wrist. The spiral staircase led to a room with doors that seemed to stretch from the floor to the ceiling. The French doors open to a grand Victorian bedroom. It was the only room in the house that was perfectly preserved; not a speck of dust. It was as if someone still lived in there. The walls are an attractive maroon and black curtains draped down to the floor. Against the wall stood an oval-shaped mirror with beautiful hand carved etchings. The detail pulls him closer.

He notices folded parchment on the mahogany desk. The aged paper was crinkled with discoloring and gothic styled calligraphy was quilled in faded ink. The author's hand appeared to tremble as he wrote, chopping and blending words as if he were rushed to finish. He held it up to the candlelight and read it aloud:

"If you're reading this, it means that I have gone from this world. I'm writing to forewarn you of the terror that lurks here for the living. The bricks were bound with unhappiness over this cursed bedrock of bones. This is not a home; it is a cold forgotten dungeon. I've been trapped here for so long that time is merely a word undefined. I do not remember the warmth of kindness or the touch of inviting love.

Why have you come to this place? Nothing awaits you here. Go now... and never return. You discovered this letter as it seems, but the truth is that it has discovered you. He found you. Your blood pumping life excites him. He will feed until you are hollow and broken. I'm truly sorry for your forsaken soul. You may not deserve this fate but it has been bestowed on you, much like it has been on me. I do not have much time and neither do you. Your body will cage the evil of this house until you ultimately succumb to the demon's influence, setting him free.

The reflection of your eyes will hide his own. Only you can see what dwells within you now. Your blood will freeze to an icy sea for the damned, who drift in the darkness of your veins. I see myself in your twinkling eyes and it saddens me. Mine looked like that once upon a time, glowing with wonder and awe. Now the light flickers dimly with the remembrance of who I used to be before darkness became me.

For the love of everything sacred, I implore, do not look up and let him in. Bit by bit, he will take your soul and break your mind. There's no escaping this torment. Do not look into this mirror, or every reflection will crack as it reveals what lives inside you.

Regretfully,

A fellow damned soul"

He fought the throbbing urge but curiosity gradually wrenched his gaze upward. The mirror broke as the demon entered his body and his eyes bled to black. He stumbles backward and awoke just as he slammed to the floor.

He immediately dials his oldest friend. "Holy shit, you wouldn't believe this nightmare I just had," he pants as reached for the aspirin. He closes the medicine cabinet but drops the phone at the sight of what stared back at him.

"...Are you there? Hello? What's going on, man? Hello..."

17

TUESDAY

"Watching my husband fade from this world was the hardest thing I ever had the misfortune to endure. Watching him slowly disappear before my eyes tore my heart from within my chest with every passing day that he hung by a thread. Though I am grateful for the final moments we shared. We lay peacefully hand in hand like we did on our first date. The drive-in was packed that night under that starry summer sky. They were showing Casablanca...our favorite. You held my hand and I knew that I was home." She taps the pen to her chin and sits down on the bed. "Hmm. How's that sound so far, honey?" she says, looking over to his unresponsive eyes.

He lies there week after week, praying for the day that her forgetful mind would neglect him long enough for death to whisk him away in the middle of a silent night. No such luck. Instead, each sunrise brings a different form of torture to his chambers.

"I want your eulogy to be heart-wrenching... not a dry eye in the room. Any suggestions for improvements?" The sharp gaze of contempt was thrown in her direction. "That's what I'm thinking too. Maybe I'll cry so people really feel the pain. Great tip."

That evening she sipped her tea while standing in front of the calendar that hung adjacent to his bed. She traced her finger along the dates and circles Tuesday in red. She turns her head to him. "How do you feel about dying on Tuesday?" The news was a blessing long overdue. He tries to hide the detection of a slight smile beginning to stretch across his chapped lips. That night he slept peacefully and dreamed of his date with the reaper.

On Tuesday, the sunrise is held captive behind gray clouds and sideways rain. Angry winds slam the shutters against the window as she towers over him with a feathered pillow in hand. She examines his breathing chest for a moment before shaking him awake. "I can't say it's been pleasant for either of us. I wanted to finish you off in the hospital on the night of your accident, but I didn't think that would be much fun." A look of disappointment washed over her face. "But now that we're finally here, I feel somewhat underwhelmed. I suppose the desire for something burns brighter than the flame of satisfaction in some cases."

His eyeballs shook with rage as he struggled to regurgitate a response. She snickers at the pathetic attempt. "Aw...are you trying to say something? Don't worry, I'll tell everyone that your last words were, I love you."

She pressed the pillow against his face and pushed. His toes curled stiffly as she leaned into her weight. She felt his heartbeat dwindling through the pillow, "Thump—thump, thump—thump...thump..." Then nothing. She sat beside his limp body and rang their daughter, who'd been expecting this call for months.

"Hello?"

"Baby," she sniffles.

"Mom, What's wrong? Is it dad?"

"Yeah, umm...Daddy's... dead. We were just laying there and then," she quivers.

The pause was painfully silent, but her daughter finally says through her tears, "I'm sure he knows how much you loved him."

18

COVEN

"The witch's coven was burned at the stake. They were forced to watch their sisters and listen to their screams as they were wrapped in the arms of dancing flames. Legend says that if you gently inhale, you can still smell their charred flesh," he says to his brother.

He shrugs with a giggle. "Shut up, dude. It's a myth. I don't know why I let you drag me out here."

The cabins of the extinct coven formed a circle and their connecting paths depicted a pentagram when viewed from above. Inside were dangling skulls, bloodstained floors, and cracked caldrons that contained remnants of children's bones.

"If you're here give us a sign!" he mocked, as he spun in a circle and looking up to the sky. "Told you, somebody built this spooky scene and made up that stupid story for Internet attention." Layers of ash and dirt were kicked up by sudden gusts of cutting wind. The breeze hissed through the trees and the clouds grew thick with black, turning daylight to darkness all at once.

He zips his jacket and stares at the clouds. "Looks like rain. Let's get out of here."

He snickers. "I knew you were scared."

"I'm not sc..." he mutters and abruptly falls to his knees. He grips his head in pain as blood dripped from his nose. Gradually, he rose to his feet and says, "I have an idea." He calmly wipes the blood from his nostril. "Let's tie you to the stake. It'd make a great picture."

His brother's face twists with confusion. "Are you okay?" he asks. "Uh, sure why not."

"Never better," he says, as he secured his brother's wrists above his head.

He makes a slightly uncomfortable face from the knots digging into his hands. "Get the shot?"

He glares blankly through his brows. "Mhm." His eyes and voice suddenly became unfamiliar. "We all died at the hands of men like you. Would you like to know how it felt?" He slid the lighter from his pocket and brushed the flame by his brother's face.

He jerked his head back from the heat. "Fuck, you burnt me! Untie me! This isn't funny anymore. I'm going to tell mom," he says, attempting to wiggle his hands free.

A sinister grin wrenched across his face as he piled twigs by his feet. "Become cleansed, my child. Feel your blood boil and your skin flake from your skull. From ashes and to ashes you shall return..."

He flicks the lighter and the flame ignites. He smiles and throws it to his feet. His eyes shimmered with the reflection of his burning brother as his shrieks eventually echo into silence.

19

DADDY

He sprung from his dreams to an excruciating throbbing in his gut. He rolled from his bed as cracks ring out from his aching limbs. He bites his knuckle and quietly weeps, careful not to disturb his sleeping wife and son in the adjacent room. His breathing grew inhumanly deep as he sat in tormented confusion. His galloping heart raced harder and faster as he crawls across the floor.

Talon-like nails burst through his fingertips and what remained did not resemble a human's hand. His razor claws ripped into the windowsill as he pulled himself to a bended knee. The full moon's spotlight shined on his face. In the window, he caught the glimpse of his reflection—the hopeless eyes once belonging to a man, a father, a husband, now glowed a haunting golden white. His teeth trickled to the floor as serrated fangs pushed through his bleeding gums.

His body was suddenly overflowing with an uncontrollable rage. A feral hunger simmered in his belly on the cusp of an eruption, and what he craved wasn't among the contents of his refrigerator. He licked his lips to the thought of his teeth tearing into the raw meat of the living, and the next room over awaited two premium cuts.

Dropping to his knees, he peered down in terror at the monstrous hands that would destroy everything he loved. He was becoming a stranger in his own mind as he felt the humanity slipping further from grasp. He tightly shut his eyes and plays tug of war with his vanishing memories. He saw their wedding; she looked so beautiful that day. He felt the loving kiss of his wife's soft lips as they held their newborn son. Then, everything collapsed to black as he sniffed the air like a bloodhound. The hunger has broken the surface, driving his only desire—to feed.

His only objective was to escape without catching their scent. He crawled down the stairs toward the door but halts in his tracks when the faint whisper of a tiny voice from the top of the landing slips into his ear. "Daddy?"

20

THE MELODY OF MIDNIGHT

"Oh my god! Thank you, thank you!" She repeatedly kissed her husband's face; just moments ago, his body laid flat and lifeless upon the shore. The rolling waves spit him up after being under for nearly five minutes. She tightly held his cold wet body close to hers. "I thought you were gone."

Days passed but things weren't exactly "normal" after the incident. "Are you coming to bed?" she says to his back as he stared idly into the darkness. He traced his fingers down the window as if he were longing for something on the other side. She called his name but he doesn't as much as flinch. She began recording the abnormal behavior in her diary as it progressively worsened.

Tonight's entry reads:

"Each night is stranger than the last. He spends more time sleepwalking than actually asleep in our bed. I felt him standing over me as I pretended to sleep. He's unraveling and I don't know what to do. The light in his eye darkens more with each glance in my direction. His gaze is cold and empty now; the one I knew felt like home. His face resembles the one I love, but he's nothing if a pale shadow of the man. Tonight I found him looking at our wedding photos, confused as to who was in them. He tossed it in the fire without a second thought and watched us smolder to ash. I'm afraid that—"

Jolting chills running down her spine interrupts the ink flow. An echo of a long-forgotten melody plays from the Baby Grand a floor below. No one had touched the piano since her ex-husband passed away. She thought she'd finally broken free from the soundtrack to her nightmares. She tiptoed down the creaking spiral staircase toward the torturous sound.

The room glowed warmly as the fireplace burns, but he was hidden in the shadows.

She nervously lingers behind him. "Why are you playing that?" The silhouette ignores her inquiry. He begins playing louder.

She screams over the noise. "How do you know that song?" He aggressively continues to slam the keys. The ferocity from his fingers sends broken keys flying into the air.

She covers her ears and crumbles to the floor. "Stop it! Stop it!" She rocks back and forth to the montage of her ex's drunken violence playing in her head; the sting if his belt upon her back and the branding scar on her thigh begin to burn as if he had just inflicted them. "Stop. Stop. Stop," she whispers.

Suddenly the room falls deaf and he whips his head in around. His empty eyes carried a ghostly stare and the voice of her dead ex-husband oozed from his mouth. "Thought you could kill me and wipe your hands clean, did you? Blood doesn't wash away that easily. You're going to have to do better than that, my love."

Her voice stiffened her with terror. "N-n-no, no, no," she stammers in disbelief.

She pushes to her feet a second too late as he pounces from the piano bench, knocking her to the floor. He holds a broken piano key to her neck. His raspy breath heats her cheek as he lowers his face down and stares into her eyes. Her screech matched the pitch of the sour stroke of a violin as he slid the jagged key into her throat. At that moment, the grandfather clock struck twelve. It gonged in cadence with deaths encroaching footsteps.

The steadfast chiming of the clock continues. "GONGGG—GONGGGG—GONGGG" rings in the background as she gargles her overflowing blood and he sits silently beside her with closed eyes, savoring the melody of midnight.

21

TWIN

"Is this a dream?" she asks the mysterious girl sitting at her bedside. It was like looking in a mirror but her reflection had a mind of its own. Studying her face, she rubs her eyes and sits against the headboard. The stranger's hair was a sandy brown and tiny freckles danced across her nose, just like hers. Their hazel eyes stared at one another. "No, it's not a dream," she responds.

She struggles to grasp the situation. "How is this possible? Who are you? Why do you look like me?"

She inches closer. "None of that matters. All you need to know is that empty creature you call 'mother,' sent me away after our birth. She had you, and that's all she wanted or needed. Two was one too many, I suppose. You were quiet and did exactly what you were told. You never screamed through the night like I did. She didn't know what was wrong with me, nor did she have the heart to care. I only know this because she told me in the coldest letter ever written. She didn't even take the time to write it by hand. I bet you get little-handwritten notes all the time..." Her eyes momentarily hung with sadness before she continues. "I shouldn't hate you but I do; such a fine line isn't it, between love and hate? To find yourself on the other side is a feeling completely unfamiliar to fathom for you, I imagine. But all of that is behind us now." With open arms, she invites her into her embrace.

She carefully leans closer. Their gaze never breaks. The familiar strangers hold one another and feel the sting of lost time as their hearts beat in unison. But then, she held tighter and tighter... and tighter as her arms moved to her neck.

"Hey, I can't breathe." The more she struggled, the harder she constricted. "Stop it, I can't breathe!"

The air deflated from her lungs as her neck bent to the brink of cracking.

"Shhhh...it's okay. Just close your eyes." She whispered as she squeezed tighter until popping sounds pierced the air. Her head falls limply onto her shoulder. "Yes, just like that," she says and kisses her softly.

She smiles, feeling the life slip from her sister's surrendering body. Her breathing stops, as does her squirming. Dragging her body into the walk-in closet, she changes into her sister's nightgown and climbs back into bed as the door handle jiggles. Her mother slowly peeks her head through the crack. "Hey, I heard a loud bump. Is everything okay?"

Her evil smirk is disguised as innocence. "Yes, mom. Everything's fine. Love you, goodnight."

She smiles back. "Get some sleep, you have school tomorrow. Love you too. Goodnight, sweetie."

22

WHEN I GROW UP

Ms. Robinson savored the hours when dusk deepened into the dark night. She'd tuck neatly into bed with a cup of Earl Grey while grading papers and tunes into the 10 o'clock news. Today's assignment was entitled "When I Grow Up." The instructions were as follows: "Tell us what you want to be when you grow up and why. After class, do one thing that relates to that career. Prepare to discuss it in class!"

She read how Sally wanted to be a nurse and Johnny had his eye on a shiny police badge. Lauren wrote, "I want to be a teacher, just like Ms. Robinson. She's my favorite!" Wiping a tear, she fondly reminisces the day she wrote something similar to her favorite teacher. She smiled as she pictured her students breathing life into their dreams. She licked her thumb and sifts through a few more. Finally, she reaches the last paper belonging to Tim, a shy and kind boy.

Tim answers, "A hunter because they're awesome! I killed our dog yesterday. I let him go into the woods then I hunted him. I broke his legs so he couldn't run anymore, and then I took off his skin. I got warm and tingly everywhere when I did it. You know when you get presents for Christmas, Ms. Robinson? That's what it felt like. I wanted to eat him, but my mom says I'm too little to use the oven. So, I just buried him there in the woods and told them he ran away. Please don't tell on me. I can't wait to do this to people instead of animals—there are a lot of people in the world so I won't run out, and they're all different so I have a lot to pick from. It would be so much fun! My daddy always tells me to do what makes me happy, so I think I'll make him proud. Maybe I'll surprise him with a gift when he gets home from work to show him how good I am! There's this new girl that moved next-door. Maybe I'll ask her to play..."

Without hesitation, her shaking hands dial Tim's parents but it goes straight to voicemail. She glances up at the TV as the anchor announces, "BREAKING NEWS! 10-year-old Timothy Daniels from Redwood Elementary brutally stabs and dismembers 9-year-old Samantha Johnson. Samantha and her parents moved into the house next-door only days prior to this tragic and horrific murder. The only thing Timothy said as he was taken into custody was, 'Ms. Robinson told me to do it.'"

She rushed to the window where police sirens bounced between houses and the flashing red and blue lights sped toward her home.

23

KNOCK, KNOCK

He stood at the window, watching at the man on the couch, whom was lost in another home renovation episode. He slips his hands into the black leather gloves and slinks toward the door as he imagines the man's story as a sad one:

He relaxed under the roof of his giant home but was empty inside despite the glamor surrounding him. His entire family died in the crash that he caused. To them, it was an innocent trip to the town fair on a sunny spring afternoon. What they didn't know was that daddy met his mistress for breakfast over mimosas and Bloody Marys earlier that morning. Ever since, he drowns in whiskey at night until he stoops into a deep and dreamless sleep.

The insurance sympathized with his situation, awarding him the lawsuit filed against the trucking company involved in the collision. All he wished for was the day that death comes knocking at his door and he answers with a smiling face. Well, he's in luck, because that day is today.

...But that wasn't his story and he didn't want to die.

So he balled his fist and raised his hand to the door "KNOCK—KNOCK," said the knuckles to the wood.

HANDS

"Do you know how hard I worked for them to feel like this?" You could hear the exhaustion in his voice as he peers down at his hand tracing a finger over the roughness of it. His sandpaper palms have become so callused over the years that a simple handshake would scrape your skin as you pulled away. Around the room are severed hands encased in trophy glass upon rows of shelves with a tiny incandescent bulb individually illuminating each of them.

"It's all about the hands...harder the hand, harder the man. Do I mistake you for someone with soft hands?" He leans across and snatches the man's hand. "As soft as a newborn's ass."

"Who are you? You have the wrong guy. I don't even know you. Let me out of here," he rebuttals.

He stares at him with disgust. "Oh, but I know you... you haven't worked a day in your life, have you? Your house in the hills came equipped with maids and landscapers, didn't it? Your 'allowance' freed you to live on your own selfish terms, eventually crumbling your soul to dust. Which bring you here..."

He backs into the shadows. With only his piercing eyes visible, he stared at the man in the cage without the slightest blink. "You get the same proposal I offered the others." He held a meaty finger in the air. "If you work for me for one year, I'll release you. You wake and sleep down here in the cellar, free to move around on your own terms, but the upstairs is off limits. The door is steel and extremely secure, so please do not try to escape; because you won't."

The man's ears perk up. "Or," says the kidnapper, in his slim blue suit repositioning his cufflinks. "I'll hack you to pieces, right here, right now, and that smooth hand of yours joins the others." He says, pointing to the vacant space on the wall.

He holds onto the cold iron bars and peeks out his face from in between. "What's the job?"

He pauses sharpening the machete and smiles. "You will help me abduct and murder anyone I instruct you to. Each week I will slide you a manila envelope. Enclosed will be the target's detailed information; pictures, schedules, and anything else to make your job as mindless as humanly possible."

The man paces in the cage, interlocking his hands behind his head and squats to the floor enthralled with contemplation. His eyes squeeze tight as he prepares to make the decision that will maintain or cease the blood to run within his veins.

He holds up a shock collar. "And if you think you can run, think again. There's enough power in here to drop an elephant. One inch too far and zap!"

At last, he opens his eyes and stands to his feet. "When do I start?"

25

TWO WAY MIRROR

"Hello?" I groan as I look over at my alarm clock. "Dude, It's 5 AM..." I hear chirping but dawn's shimmering rays had yet to peak through my blinds.

"Hey. I know, sorry. Could you head over here?"

His voice sounded shaky and I could tell he hasn't slept. "Yeah, of course. What's up, man?"

"Just hurry."

"What's wrong?" I ask, but he hangs up before I could pry any deeper.

Damn, it's freezing out here. I knock a few times and wait at the door watching my own breath. He slowly cracks open the door. "Come in," he says, yanking my shirt toward him.

I could barely see anything once I entered the room. "Why's it so dark in here? And why are you acting so strange?"

He deflected the questions. "I need you to do something for me..."

I'm intrigued...yet frightened. I've known him for fifteen years and he's never been one to drop his prideful drawbridge, not even to ask for a favor. "Anything, you know that," I say.

He sat with me under the amber light in the dim kitchen. He took the seat opposite me and I finally was able to see his face. It wasn't the one that I remember growing up with. His sunken bloodshot eyes reached out in pain. Something behind them screamed for help, but his stare was blank. "Kill me," he says.

I laugh. "We've all had tough days, buddy. Let's talk about it over a stogie and a smooth single malt." I stand from the table and walk through over to the minibar. "Hey, do you know this mirror's broken?"

His feet crunch over the broken glass as he approaches me. "Yes."

His vagueness has become irritating. "Any particular reason why?"

His whisper jumps to a roar. "Are you going to help me or not?" He grabs a sharp piece of broken mirror and holds it to his throat. "I'll do it myself if you don't!" Blood drips down his wrist as the glass cuts into his palm.

I hold out my hands but hesitate to move toward him. "Whoa, Calm down! Tell me what's going on with you. Put down the glass."

He slowly steps closer. "Whatever I do, wherever I go, he's there. I'm afraid to blink because, in that instance of black, I see those horrible eyes and grotesque smile. He hides in the cracks of my mind and only shows himself through my reflection. The lines between his twisted thoughts and my own blur more with each passing glance. I can feel him taking over. Help me, please."

I politely suggest it's a figment of his imagination. "Maybe you should talk to somebody, a professional I mean. Have you been taking your meds?"

He points the shard at me. "Fuck the meds! I'm not crazy! This is real. I'm telling you he's real."

I fear the elasticity of his reality has stretched to its breaking point. So I play along, "Okay, he's real. What does he want? Why you?"

He found solace that somebody was finally listening. "Remember when I found that letter? It told me this would happen."

"That wasn't real! You told me it was a dream," I scream and feel the veins bulge from my neck.

He lunges, tackling me to the floor and holds the sharp edge to my throat. "He's real! Look into his eyes and tell him that you believe!" I struggled under his weight as I hold away his arm, but my hand slips from his slick wrist. The shard punctures my neck. I spit blood as I whisper, "Please...stop."

At last, the demon's eyes reveal themselves. Their blackened emptiness stares down at me with pleasure, as the stranger stabbing my chest laughs through his grin.

26

NEIGHBORS

He enjoyed his steak and eggs from the comfort of the porch as the rising sun kissed his cheek; a routine he kept for twenty-five years. The daily group of cardio conscious mothers waves to him in unison as they speed walk passed his house and greet him with a pleasant, "Good morning!"

"Beautiful morning, ladies," he says, with a smile and a wave.

Each Halloween he transformed his home into an extravagant haunted house for all to enter if they dared, and this All Hallows Eve was no different. His face beams with satisfaction as he stared at his creation and prepared for the evening ahead. Children came and went, one after another as the night stretched on. Everyone knew that he closed his doors at midnight, marking the end of his haunted attraction. As he was closing the door and blowing out the jack-o-lanterns, two trick-or-treaters mosey up to the base of his steps at 11:59. One was dressed as Batman and the other as Clark Kent. "Still open?" They ask, with hopeful eyes.

"Sure is," he says, proceeding to close the door behind them. "Each room offers something scarier than the last. Have fun, boys."

They excitedly scurry through the house while he lurked slightly out of sight. He hovered by one final door as the children emerged from the last "Room of Fright," as he called them. "Want to see something cool?" he asks. Of course, they do, so he outstretched a bony wrinkled hand and pointed down the dark staircase. They roam the basement unimpressed by the lack of decoration as rats squeak and scatter at the sound of wandering footsteps. Only the diminishing fire of a rusted coal-burning furnace flickered in the dirty cellar. His innocent gaze turns menacingly devious as his silent feet slithered closely behind their heels. The sound of his panting caused the hair on the children's necks to whisper, "It's time to go."

"Thanks, mister. This was really scary." He says, as his feet shift toward the exit.

The old man placed a hand on the boy's shoulder. "You're welcome, kiddo," but as they turned to leave, he grabs Batman by the cape and heaves him into the furnace.

Clark Kent frantically climbs the stairs but is forcefully tugged back down by his ankle. The old man stomps his foot on the boy's chest as he hits the ground. He cackles as the delicate ribs crack under the pressure of his boot until his body gradually deflates. The screams from the furnace finally fall silent as he runs his fingers through his wispy white hair.

The following morning, he emerges from his home with a fresh plate of steak and eggs, after neatly stacking the boys' chopped bodies in the freezer. Concerned parents walk the street with panicking voices that rose above the blackbirds' morning songs. They cupped their hands to their mouths and yelled from the curb. "Have you seen our boys? Did they stop in last night?"

He washed down the meat with a swig of juice and cleared his throat. "Sorry, rude to speak with a full mouth. No ma'am, but I'll keep my eyes peeled and call you if I happen to see them" he says, as he cut into her son's medium-rare filet and sucks the blood off his fingers.

A lone mother trails behind the others and walks up to the porch. "I saw you."

He sips his drink again. "Pardon me?"

"I saw what you did to them in the basement." He stared at her blankly. He knew this day would come eventually. He wondered if they'd shove him to the front of death row or let him rot in a cell.

"Can you do something for me?" She said, in a quiet tone.

He looks at her with defeated eyes. "I'm listening..."

She smiles. "Leave me leftovers?"

He smiles back.

27

BLACK COFFEE

She stopped in each morning for her French vanilla Frappuccino with a caramel heart drizzle, specially made by the kind-eyed barista. She was the love of his life. She just didn't know it yet. His heart melted from the heat of her eyes, as she'd say, "The regular," with a wink and a smile. Her hair left the aroma of sweet apple cinnamon lingering in the air when she turned to leave. He knew exactly when to inhale to catch the scent of every strand as it flipped over her shoulder. He'd always have something witty prepared as they parted ways, but chokes on his words as they inch toward his lips.

So there he stood, trapped behind the counter that divided their hearts once more as he watches her exit and thinks, "Until next time, my love."

He daydreamed of handing her that cup as their fingers gingerly brush and he'll say, "You look beautiful today." He snaps out of the empty stare with a gentle nudge from his manager. "Watch it, you're over pouring the java."

"Shit. Sorry, zoned out for a second."

"You're always zoned out. Just clean it up."

"Yes, sir."

The next morning, he stared into the mirror with noble intent, as he brushed his freshly trimmed hair and slid on his sleek new glasses. "Today is the day," he says to his reflection.

She strolled in with the rays of the sunrise to the sound of the door's jingling bells. He watched her walk past the counter without as much as a friendly nod. "Did I do something wrong?" he thinks, as she sat at the table on the other side of the shop. Not a minute later, a man walks over, taking the seat opposite her and smiles.

His body ignites at the sight of the stranger. Sweat beads above his brows. He screams internally, "No! No! No! Who's that? This is MY day! This is all wrong."

He releases his shaking white-knuckled fist squeezed at his side and cheerfully walks up to the table. "Good morning! The usual?"

She smiles big. "Hey, you! Good morning and yep, the usual. Wow, new glasses. Looking spiffy!"

His smitten heart swells with joy. "Thanks," he says, and immediately regrets not returning the compliment.

He begins to ask the man, "And for y-?"

"Black coffee," he interrupts.

Rage instantly replaced his joy. Instead of scooping a spoon into his eye socket and force feeding it to him like he envisioned, he smiles pleasantly. "Sure thing. Coming right up."

He returns with the orders. "Can I get you anything else?" He imagines splashing the piping hot coffee onto the man's face and watching his smooth skin melt.

"Nope. All set, boss. How about you?" He looks at her. "Did I tell you that you look beautiful today?"

He was enraged by the words stolen from his mouth but appeared as calm as a breezeless sea.

He grips the pen in his pocket and presses the point to his thumb until it punctures flesh. "Focus, focus, focus," he reiterates in his brain. The pain deters his sinister thoughts. "Have a great day," he says, smirking through his heartbreak.

She smiles back. "You too, Clark Kent." She turned to leave, but the overpowering stench of musky cologne cloaked her apple cinnamon sweetness. He quivers with madness as he watched them walk out the door. And just like that, his dream was burned to ash.

He taps his manager on the shoulder. "I have to go to the bathroom."

"I'll watch the counter."

He snuck out the back and jumped in his car. He followed his girl back to the stranger's apartment where they laughed and flirted the morning away. His hands firmly grip the steering wheel as he watches the two through the window, sick to the sight of romantic gazes.

"See you soon," he says, with a final glance and peels off.

He returns at nightfall and stood at the stranger's landing. He knocks three times and the man opens the door, pleasantly greeted with a chloroform cloth. His eyes slowly open to the sight of the barista's face just inches from his own. "Good morning, sleepyhead."

His voice slurs as he wakes. "You're that coffee guy... from earlier? What the fuck is going on?" He squints from the blinding light. "Untie me," he says, wiggling his wrists that are strapped to the chair.

He shakes his head. "I don't think you're in the position to be making demands. Plus you can't just give me what I want... I'm going to have to take it."

He spits at his feet. "I'm going to kill you, freak."

"Might be difficult from where you're sitting." He presses the knife to his chest. "What's her hair smell like?"

Confusion scrunches across his brow. "What?"

He thrusts the knife in. "Wrong answer. What color are her eyes?" The man lets out a painful grunt. "Errrrr, wrong again." He stabs him twice more and watches the deep red soak through his white tee shirt.

"Where is she tonight?"

It suddenly clicks. "She'll be here... at nine... just let me go," he musters to say.

His watch shows 8:30. "Then I guess I better hurry." He carefully aligns the blade to his jaw and surgically slices around his face. He peels the skin inch-by-inch until the screams from the faceless man eventually end.

"Perfect fit," he says, pressing the flesh to his face as droplets of blood drip from the warm skin. The doorbell rings from the floor above. "You look beautiful tonight," he says to the mirror, preparing himself to greet his girl.

28

ORPHANS

Her life was forever changed on that ordinary Sunday in December. It was a roadside robbery gone wrong on their way home from a day trip into town. Both of her parents were left to bleed in a snowdrift while she was home reading by the fire. With those two gunshots on that snowy evening, an orphan was born. She was left alone in the forgotten farmhouse through the brutal blizzards of the long and dark winter.

After the livestock froze to death, she scoured the house from sun-up to sundown for breadcrumbs to eat. On a particularly frigid week, she noticed that she was fresh out of firewood and books to burn. She wore four layers of clothes while she'd lie by the hole in the wall night after night waiting for a snack to crawl out. As her tired eyes began creeping closed, a tiny field mouse poked its head out. She snatched it up before it could flinch. She sunk her teeth into the squealing rodent and devoured every last bite from head to tail. She peered down at her bloody hands and vowed from that day forward she'd never let an orphaned child walk through life alone. As the snow thawed each spring, she traveled to neighboring towns search for homeless children to provide refuge for. Now fifty years later, she still tends to dozens of smiling young faces under that very same roof.

She kissed the children's foreheads as she tucked them in. "Lights out everyone, big day tomorrow at the festival. Don't forget to wear your uniforms." The children woke to crowing roosters as the sun peeked over the horizon. They trotted down the staircase and out the door in black cloaks and skeleton masks. They arrived at The Day of the Dead festival with clear instructions for the "rescue mission," as she liked to call them: Kill the parents. Collect the children. They were taught that love demanded sacrifice and their souls would remain unblemished if they were "rescuing" children from horrible families. A sense of purpose replaced their guilt as the outings grew easier with every stab and slice.

With knives in hand, they split into pairs and searched for separated families. They picked off vulnerable parents one by one and lured the cornered children under their protection. "Come play with us," they'd say to the children who were unaware of their parents' demise.

Fear captivated the newly orphaned children as they wondered about their folks. "Where's my mommy and daddy? They were supposed to meet me when the ride was over."

"They don't want you anymore. They left you here, but it's okay we'll take care of you," said the oldest of the bunch with a blood dripped knife behind his back. The three lost children they collected wanted their parents back but they needed to go with the skeletons if they were to live, so the choice was made. They held hands as they walked home through the cornfield, leaving the blood of their families steaming in the chill of the night.

The old woman stood on the porch with open arms. "Welcome home! Come in and get yourselves warm. Your new brothers and sisters will be helping you from now on." She points to the staircase. "The other children know the routine so just follow them. Wash up, and put on the clothes I folded for you inside the rooms. "

The children return to the dining room in their black cloaks where supper awaits. The spread included pizza, cookies, ice cream, and everything a child could ever dream of. "Eat up. Tomorrow starts your new life. We're going to change the world, my children."

29

MESSAGE IN A BOTTLE

He stood amid the salt-stained shoreline where moonlit water kissed his feet. He rolled up the paper and slid it carefully into the clear glass bottle. He bent down and scooped a handful of sand and watched as the golden grains slip through his fingers. A tear escapes his eye, dropping into the deep blue. He kissed the bottle and ties it to the wrist of the man beside him. "I need you to deliver this for me."

The tortured, bleeding man looks at him with dying eyes. "No," he mumbles.

"You took her from me and now I need you to take this to her. Even trade I'd say." He doused him in gasoline and struck the lighter against his jeans. "Two choices—get very hot or get very wet. Either way, this is the end of the road for you."

The man began walking up to the surf-battered shore. He trudged through the sinking sand, deeper and farther until he merged into the whitecaps becoming one with the black watered ocean. He sat in the dry sand and wept as he watched the man who murdered his wife carry the goodbye he never got the chance to give.

A week from that night, the bottle washed ashore and into the hands of a young woman; she unrolled the letter and her eyes traveled from line to line. "Honey, come read what I just found."

He wraps his arms around her from behind and kisses her head. "What is it?"

"A letter... to his dead wife." She points to the water. "I saw it bobbing there in the shallows." He reads it aloud.

"My Love,

I shiver from the absence of your touch as I dreamt of your hand held tight within my clutch. I longed for the riptide to drag me under when I was awoken by the booming thunder. That sleep was a sliver of heaven, where I learned my final lesson-In a permanent slumber is where I'll find you drifting beneath the ocean blue. Cotton candy skies gave way to stars, as I stand under the moon afar. My heart drowned with you that night as I felt it sinking out of sight. It's buried with you in that watery grave, which is now the only place I crave. Here I walk with sandy toes, into the sea as the cold wind blows. There is no life without you above, so below to you is where I long to go. Until we meet again but until then, rest and dream of me my love... until then."

Crashing waves intercept the mournful silence as they stared into the bleeding orange horizon. "I wonder what happened to them," she whispers to her husband.

A man walked up beside them to admire the sunset. "Looks like I'll have to deliver this myself. If you want something done right, do it yourself," he says to the couple as he takes the bottle and walks out to where the sun meets the ocean.

30

NIGHTMARES & DAYDREAMS

It's been months without a peaceful sleep—an hour here, an hour there is the most he managed to escape with. He's trapped in that wretched place the second his drowsy eyes give way to fatigue. Night terrors invade his days and warp reality with fantasy. He wondered what that word even meant to him anymore. If "reality" is simply an awareness of our conscious present, his lucid nightmares certainly fit the criteria. He lived awake in both worlds, creating a blended labyrinth of horror unable to tell fact from fiction. He walks the streets with dread that his deepest fears would manifest out from passing shadows.

He enjoyed a midnight coffee at the diner across the street when insomnia ruled his mind. Tonight was one of those nights. After mindlessly staring at the ceiling for hours, he carefully slid out of bed mindful of his sleeping wife. He walked into the diner and over to his usual spot. He sat at the red leather booth by the window, under the neon "Open 24 Hours," sign. His thousand-mile stare was broken by a woman's voice. "Warm you up?" she said, pouring steaming coffee into his mug.

His dark circled eyes stare at her rotting face. Pieces of flesh flaked into his coffee and puss oozed from the open sores covering her body.

She felt slightly insulted by his disgusted gaze. "Geez. I know I don't have on makeup tonight. Go easy on me."

He rubbed his eyes and her face returned to its smooth and unblemished form. "Sorry," he laughs. He stirred in the sugar and subtly checked his coffee for skin flakes. "I'm not myself tonight. Thanks for the joe."

He returns home shortly after his coffee and tucks into bed. It's now 3:17 AM and lays awake, watching silent reruns of the same late night movies. Then, "BOOM!" A crashing thud from the living room startles him out of his trance. The sound has footsteps now and grew louder with every step approaching the door only feet from where he lays. He thinks to jump up and lock it, but the hinges squeak before he could move a muscle. The shadowy figure engulfed the entire doorway...just watching. Its penetrating red eyes were locked on him.

The waves of panic send him cowering under the covers. He stills his breath and pretends to be invisible. It walks slow and steady, one soft footstep after another. The creature reaches out its hand and rips back the covers. A black serpent slithers from the shadow down into his throat. He yanks the snake from his esophagus with both hands, squeezing it limp. His adrenaline-charged hands continue to choke and in that final moment of rage, he snaps awake. He frees his constricting grip to reveal the lifeless gaze of his wife's eyes as he straddles her strangled corpse.

31

66.6

He turns to his friend. "Wait for me. If I'm not out in twenty, come get me."

He pushed open the heavy wooden door just enough to slide in. Chills traveled down his spine as it slammed from behind. He hesitantly steps into the darkness. His heart was beating so rapidly that it almost hummed. "Where were all the cobwebs and dust-covered furniture," he thought, as he looked around at a house that was all too familiar. His feet crept over the worn welcome mat that he's tread over a million times before. It wasn't just any house that he entered; he stood frozen in the middle of the house he grew up in. "No fucking way," he says, noticing his mother's crystal collection in corner curio.

His shoes climbed the same stairs that he scurried down every Christmas morning since he learned to walk. His family photos still hung to the right of the staircase, exactly like they used to. He pauses as his hand touches the knob attached to the white door at the top of the landing. He shuts his eyes and lightly slaps his cheek. "This isn't real. This isn't real," he repeats under his breath.

His twists the knob and studies every inch of the museum to his childhood. The posters, the smell, and his Spiderman comforter...it was all there. His attention shifts to the faint scratching heard from the windowsill. As he inched closer, he saw the cracked nails and bleeding hands that hung by a thread.

The boy screams up to him. "Help me!"

He hesitates, but instinct forced him to grab an arm. "I got you. Just hold on!" His fingers begin slipping. Then, the radio sitting on his dresser flash tunes to station 66.6. Ear-splitting static fills the room and a raspy voice clears the fuzz. "Are you sure you want to do that? How will saving him change your future? No more only child treatment...he was always the favorite wasn't he?"

He snaps at the voice. "What are you talking about? You don't know anything."

"Oh, but I know everything. I know that you feel like you were nothing and that you're nothing still. Even with him gone, you still live in his shadow, don't you?"

His face turns bitter as the war between redemption and temptation rage inside him yet again. His mind actively played the scenario of a second chance at that day, and here it is.

"Or you can let him go...like you did before. No one would know. Walk out a free man like nothing ever happened." Growing impatient, the radio's volume amplifies. "What's it going to be? Make your choice. Do it now!"

His hand slips another inch and yells back at the radio. "Shut the fuck up!"

He looked down at their fingers sliding further from grip and whispers, "I'm sorry," as he lets go and stares into his baby brother's eyes. He again plummets to the concrete, and left is his brother wallowing in a sea of guilt once more. He jammed himself into a corner and his eyes catch a flickering glare from across the room.

"You chose wisely," snickers the voice.

"It was an accident...I didn't mean it," he says through his whooping cry.

He held his hands over his ears. "This isn't real. Get out of my head. This isn't real."

"Does the aching your heart feel real? Do your tears not moisten your cheek? Is that not the same knife used to whittle sticks into spears as a child? Now say it... you wanted him dead."

He grinds his teeth and admits, "...I wanted him dead."

"I'm sorry, what did you say?"

"...I wanted him to die."

The voice sighs in relief. "Ahhh, doesn't that feel better? Now, do the right thing."

The glimmering edge of a red-handled pocketknife sat on his dresser beside the radio. He crawls to the blade and grabs it with a shaking palm. The voice quakes with anticipation. "Yesss, now ssslice," it hissed.

He carved his wrists to the bone and sat in the river of heartbroken blood. "I'm sorry, I'm sorry, I'm sorry, I'm sorry...I'm...sorr..." His whispers fade to silence, as his guilty heart beats no longer.

His friend's voice echoed from the foyer. "Hey, It's been twenty minutes! Where are you?" He follows the trail of trickling blood up the stairs. He swung the door open to find him lying lifeless and alone in a dark corner of an abandoned house with boarded windows, with "I'm sorry," carved into his arms.

32

ONE MILLION VIEWS

Suddenly the darkness had footsteps. "Marco... Marco? I can't find you unless you say Polo," said a calm and chilling voice.

A breathy whisper responds from trembling lips. "...P-p-polo."

The feet creaked down the last step before hitting the cement floor. The air breathes thick with fear as the man crept closer. He flips a switch that cracks the silence, illuminating a scraggly man strapped to an autopsy table. The light was at the man's back as he stood over his victim, shrouding his face in shadow. "This letter opener was my wife's," he said, twirling it between his fingers.

He admires the sharpness of the edge. "She refused to rip envelopes with her hands. She just loved that crisp sound of the blade gliding through paper...rrrrrrip!" He says, pretending to slice open an invisible envelope. "Just like the sound of it slicing through her throat. Shall we begin?"

He carefully aligns the blade under the man's index fingernail. "Shh shh shh. Now there, don't squirm or you'll make a mess." He tightens his whimpering lips as he prepares for agony.

"That's better."

He jammed the knife in with his hand like a hammer to a chisel. Blood dripped down the side of his finger as silent screams groan from behind his grinding teeth. "That wasn't so bad, huh?" He lets out a voice-cracking shriek as his nail is pried from his finger. "One down, nine to go."

After plucking away each fingernail, he tapped the knife against his toes. "I'm exhausted. How about something easier?" He rifles through the toolbox and returns with tin snips. He rests his big toe between the freezing blades. "This little piggy went to the market," he says, snipping through the flesh and bone like warm butter. Blood spouted from his leaking toe as he flailed and screamed.

"See, you made a mess! I told you not to squirm. Let's clean you off." He walked over to the sink and touched the back of his hand to the scalding water, "perfect." He slowly poured it onto the fresh wounds, melting everything it touched. "Sorry for the splashing, I'll get you something to dry off." He slid a square of grainy sandpaper from his apron and scrubbed the man's blistering skin that effortlessly peeled from his legs with each pass.

His voice was hoarse from screaming. "Please. Stop. I'll do anything. I'll give you whatever you want. Don't kill me," said the raspy whisper.

He sighs. "I'm not going to kill you." The man's eyes twinkle with a shimmer of hope.

"Let me rephrase that...I'm not going to kill you, but you are going to die. After this, I'm taking you for a long walk on the beach. You'll live long enough to experience every second of misery as you sink under the midnight sky. You'll peer up at the stars as you struggle to swim, but their sparkle will drift further from sight until blackness cloaks your view. The frigid water will squeeze your lungs with each soaking breath. That's what you did to the woman from the video, wasn't it?"

He walks toward the flashing red light at the foot of the table. "One million views," he says, detaching the camera from the tripod. "One million people tuned into the live stream of my wife's torture on this exact table. I wonder how many are watching yours right now..."

33

THE PHOTOGRAPHER

"Amazing, Christine. Just like that," he says, snapping shots from different angles. She laid outstretched on a white loveseat in black lace lingerie and red-bottomed pumps. The soft lighting caressed her curves as her hypnotic eyes seduced the lens.

Pleased with his work, he lowers the camera from his eye. "Perfect. I'll develop these straight away, stay by the phone. You're going to love how these turn out!"

"I'm excited! Thank you so much." She wrapped herself in a silk robe and scurries off to the changing room.

It was just after sunset when he stood amidst the red glow of the darkroom and hung the photos on the drying line. Pictures of various women were pinned upon his wall of admiration from previous boudoir shoots. He reached for the scissors and started slicing through a photo catalog of former clients. He flipped through the book and removed a face from here, a leg from there, and added them to the collage of his picture-perfect woman pinned up on his cork board. He stares at the compilation of body parts and smiles. The only thing missing was a pair of eyes. There was a notebook sitting on the desk under his creation. In it contained a detailed list of women's names and what parts of them he would collect:

"Cindy- Head.

Nina- Legs.

Brooke- Torso.

Rose- Arms.

Delores- Feet."

He slid the pen from behind his ear, pressed it to the blank space and writes, "Christine- Eyes."

He dials Christine and it rings twice before the cheerful voice answers. "Hey! Wow, that was fast!"

He carefully inspects the scalpel and tongs that he'll be using to harvest her minty green eyes. "Why don't you swing by and take a look. I'd email them to you, but nothing quite compares to the intimacy of holding them up close and personal."

"Be right over!"

"Can't wait."

34

PERSPECTIVE

Hers

The same man held the door for me at precisely the same time every day after work, and there he was again. "Gentlemen are few and far between these days," I said to him. It was sweet, knowing there were still chivalrous men in the world, the type to lay down their jacket in a muddy puddle for a lady.

The clouds reflected a pink hue among the darkening blue of sundown as I pulled into my parking garage. I got out of my car and began walking when a voice from behind echoed in my direction. "Didn't know you lived here too," it said. I turn to see the smiling face of my handsome door holding gentleman.

I giggle and flip my hair with a coy smile. "Wow, small world! Have a great night. See you tomorrow?"

"You too. Yep, same time same place," he replies with a wink. That familiar face was starting to grow on me as if the fluttering butterflies in my stomach weren't enough. I'm still new to the city; I could use a friend and who knows where it could go from there. My lips involuntarily smile as I enter the elevator when I hear, "Hold the door!" I stick out my hand, and low and behold, in walks my door holding knight in a three-piece suit.

I blush and trip over my tongue. Thankfully he was quick on his feet. "Looks like the roles have reversed," he said with a delicate smile and laugh as we watched the doors close the beginning to our fairytale story.

His

Here she comes again. I wonder what her insides would look like on a kebab. I bet her bones would make for a beautiful chandelier, look at how long and slender they are. I smile at her as I hold the door like I always do. I have her schedule down to the second now. Sometimes I'm even a bit early. She mutters something or other about a gentleman, but all I can hear are the sound of her teeth tinkling as wind chimes dangling from my balcony.

I take a shortcut home to our apartment building so I can beat her to the parking garage. I bought a spot right near hers. She's right on time, "Didn't know you lived here too," I say to her. She spins her head and those silky blonde locks move with her; I can't wait to add them to my braided quilt. She speaks so softly that I can't quite hear what she says. Except for, "Have a great night and see you tomorrow." I lie through my teeth and say, "You too and yep, same place same time." Knowing that she most definitely will not be having a "great night," and she certainly will not be seeing much of anything tomorrow.

I hid behind a wall in the lobby until I saw her enter the elevator. "Hold the door," I yell as I jog.

"Looks like the roles have reversed," I say playfully as she holds the door for me. We smile as they close, sending us up but only one of us will ever come down.

THE END

AFTERWORD FROM THE AUTHOR

Dearest reader,

From the bottom of my heart, thank you for reading Melodies of Midnight. My name is Dave, and it is my utmost pleasure to meet you. I sincerely hope you enjoyed these twisted tales, and I hope they echo in the back of your mind when you hear a bump in the night.

The characters in these stories are humans just like you and me, but humans can be viscous creatures, can't we? The monsters from these tales hide in plain sight; dressed in familiar clothes, say similar things, but none of us are quite the same underneath our perceived exteriors, are we?

This book is apart of you now. Share the stories, pass them down, or keep them as your own little secret to read in the dark. As you go forth experiencing the wonder and terror of tomorrow's unknown, remember what I told you in the beginning—Nothing is ever as it seems.

Sweet dreams,

David A. Volpe

SYNOPSES

1. Blue Eyes: A man falls in love with a beautiful young woman with piercing blue eyes, but the romance isn't quite working out.

2. Hummingbird: A couple plans a romantic weekend getaway. He nervously prepares for the night he intends on proposing to the love of his life but doesn't go as expected.

3. Into the Woods: A boy moves to a new town and starts his first day of school. His new friends tell him to run through the woods, away from the clown who will "get him."

4. **Cherry Wine:** Two women argue in a restaurant bathroom over a murderous plot, but only one exits.
5. **Static:** A stranger breaks into a woman's house. She hides, waiting for him to leave.

6. **Puppet Master:** A man lives under strings controlled by his wife, but things are about to change.

7. **Red Christmas**: This family's picture-perfect Christmas doesn't stay that way for long.

8. **Dinner Party:** A cannibalistic aristocrat, new to the neighborhood, throws a dinner party for his neighbors.

9. **Good Samaritan:** A woman stops her car to help a shy boy, sitting alone in a puddle.

10. **The Devil's Door:** A man stands before an ominous black gate dubbed, "The Devil's Door."
11. **Awake:** A man wakes to find himself buried alive without reason.

12. **Night Shift**: He starts his new job at the graveyard and learns what the night shift is all about.

13. **Black Widow:** On a winter night, a woman attends a party and catches the eye of a handsome stranger.

14. **Lake House:** Newlyweds move into a beautiful lakefront home, where strange things begin to happen.

15. **Wanted:** A killer posts a "Wanted" ad for a willing victim to adhere to his terms and conditions.

16. **The Letter:** A man discovers a letter that contains an unsettling message.

17. **Tuesday:** A woman prepares to say goodbye to her husband, who dies on a Tuesday.

18. **Coven:** Two brothers travel into the woods where it's said to be home to the coven that was burned at the stake during the witch trials.

19. **Daddy:** A man struggles with a transformation that threatens the safety of his family and those around him.

20. **The Melody of Midnight:** A woman's husband comes back to life. He begins acting strange since his second chance at life.

21. **Twin:** Twins meet each other for the first time after being separated at birth.

22. **When I Grow Up:** A teacher reads through today's assignment entitled, "What do you want to be when you grow up?"

23. **Knock, Knock**: An unsuspecting man gets a late night visit.

24. **Hands:** A man obsessed with hands has an offer to make.

25. **Two Way Mirror:** A man's soul hangs in the balance as he asks his friend for help.

26. **Neighbors:** Halloween night doesn't disappoint at the haunted house of an elderly neighbor.

27. **Black Coffee:** The barista at a local coffee shop struggles to express his feeling to the girl of his dreams.

28. **The Orphanage:** The orphanage managed by an old woman holds a dark secret within its walls.

29. **Message in a Bottle:** A heartbroken man delivers a message to his wife.

30. **Nightmares & Daydreams:** A man suffers from terrible nightmares, taking his insomnia to a terrifying level.

31. **66.6:** He wanders into a mysterious house that tests his conscience.

32. **One Million Views:** One million people watch a brutal torture on a live streaming video.

33. **The Photographer:** A boudoir photographer starts an interesting side project.

34. **Perspective:** The tale of the same day is told from the perspective of two different people.

CONNECTING THE DOTS
SPOILERS AHEAD

As noted at the beginning of this book, certain stories connect to others. Below is a list of those stories and how they relate.

Black Widow - Cherry Wine: Cherry Wine is told from the perspective of a sweet woman suffering from dissociative identity disorder, and shares her body with a murderous psychopath. Black Widow is told from the murderess' side.

One Million Views – Message in a Bottle: He may have been satisfied in the moment, but nothing will ever bring back his wife or his heart.

The Devil's Door – 66.6: The same man who walks up to and through the ominous gate is the same man who was psychologically tormented inside that abandoned house at the end of the cobblestone path in The Devil's Door.

Dinner Party – Neighbors: Dinner party is the prequel to Neighbors. Our peppered with gray-haired cannibal moves into the house at the end of the road 25 years before he becomes the old white-haired man, who kills/eats two children on Halloween.

Hands - Knock, Knock: After the man in the cage from Hands accepts the job offer, his target is the man from Knock, Knock. The stories he creates for his "clients" are the only thing that holds his humanity by a thread...for now.

Tuesday – The Melody of Midnight: The man on the end of the smothering in Tuesday returns for his post-mortem revenge in The Melody of Midnight.

The Letter – Two Way Mirror: The same man waking from his dream in "The Letter," finds himself tormented to the point of suicide. Is it real or is it all in his head? You decide.

Made in the USA
San Bernardino, CA
19 February 2019